W9-ATL-859

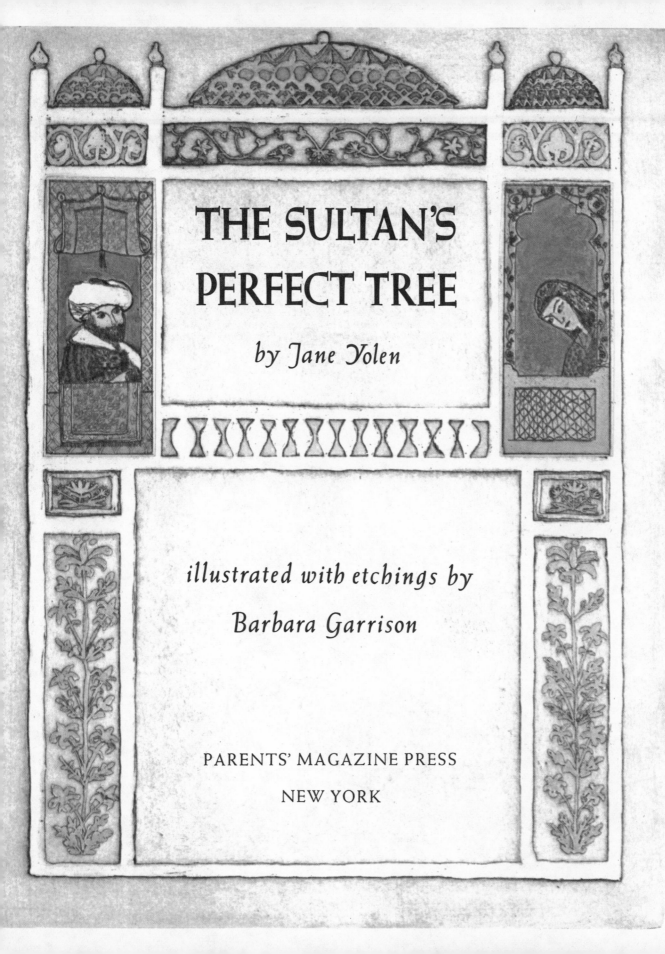

THE SULTAN'S PERFECT TREE

by Jane Yolen

illustrated with etchings by

Barbara Garrison

PARENTS' MAGAZINE PRESS

NEW YORK

Text copyright © 1977 by Jane Yolen
Illustrations copyright © 1977 by Barbara Garrison
All rights reserved
Printed in the United States of America

Library of Congress Cataloging in Publication Data
Yolen, Jane H
    The sultan's perfect tree.
    SUMMARY: A sultan wants everything around him to be
perfect until he realizes that perfect things don't grow
or change.
    [1. Perfection—Fiction] I. Garrison, Barbara.
II. Title.
PZ7.Y78Su   [E]   76-18096
ISBN 0-8193-0864-1   ISBN 0-8193-0865-X lib. bdg.

For my almost perfect and very real Adam
J. Y.

and for Brian
B. G.

HERE WAS ONCE A SULTAN who loved perfection. In his palace he would allow only the most perfect things. Each fruit that he ate had to be without blemish. Each cup that he drank from had to be without flaw. The servants who waited upon him were always handsome or beautiful, with features set exactly in their faces, and limbs not an inch too long or short. Everything, in fact, was perfect.

One day in the fall, the sultan was looking out at his perfect garden. Seven gardeners saw to it that only the most beautiful plants were allowed to grow. Every morning they would trim off broken branches or dying leaves and replace any flower that was in danger of drooping.

In the center of the garden grew a tree. It had been planted by the grandfather of the sultan and was tall and straight and kept perfectly shaped.

As the sultan gazed out his window at the garden, his eyes most naturally fell on the tree at its center. Suddenly, a swift wind blew into the garden, more savage than any wind before it. The tree bowed and swayed, its leaves shaking and shivering, turning up first the red side, then the gold. As the sultan watched, many of the leaves were ripped loose from their stems and blown to the ground. Soon the tree looked patchy, as if painted in by a trembling hand.

"It is not perfect," the sultan said angrily to himself. Then more loudly he cried out, *"It is not perfect!"*

At his cry, the servants came running. "What is it, O perfect one," they asked, for so they had been instructed to address him.

"That!" the sultan answered angrily, pointing out the window at the offending tree.

"It is but a tree," said the newest serving girl, daughter of the chief steward. Though she was beautiful to look at, she was not yet perfect in her conduct.

"But it is no longer perfect," said the sultan. "I want a perfect tree. A perfect autumn tree."

"How is that to be done?" inquired the chief steward, for he knew well enough to let the sultan give instructions.

"Call the gardeners!" ordered the sultan.

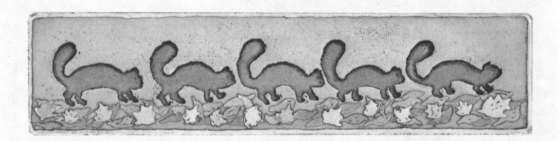

The seven gardeners came at a run. They caught the falling leaves in willow baskets and carried them out of sight. They plucked the remaining leaves from the tree, climbing to the top on shaky wooden ladders. But they were not quick enough for the sultan.

He turned away from the window and cried, "It is *not perfect*. Take down the tree."

The chief steward was so shocked, he forgot for a moment to be perfect. "But it is your grandfather's tree," he stammered. "It was planted on the day your father was born."

And because his grandfather had been perfectly wise in all that he did, the sultan said, "Then I shall not cut it down."

"What shall be done, then?" asked the chief steward, once again the perfect servant.

"Close up my window to the garden," said the sultan. "And send for the best painter in my kingdom. Have him paint me a perfect autumn tree on a screen. Set the screen before the window. Then when I let my gaze fall that way, I shall always see a perfect tree."

So it was done. The best painter in the kingdom was sent for. He labored seven days until he had painted a magnificent autumn tree, upright, tall, and completely red-gold.

"Perfect," said the sultan when the painter was done.

Two servants set the screen before the window and the painter was rewarded handsomely.

For several months the sultan was delighted. Often he would remark to his chief steward, "*There* is a perfect autumn tree."

eanwhile, outside it had grown cold. The winter snows came swirling down from the far mountains. All around, the world lay still and white—everywhere but on the sultan's autumn tree.

One day, as the sultan sat drinking his tea, the newest young serving girl came into the room. She carried a bowl in which winter branches were perfectly arranged and set in hard-packed snow.

"O perfect master," she said, "pray accept this representation of the season."

The sultan looked from the bowl to the screen, where his perfect autumn tree stood, splendid and red-gold. His face grew thoughtful. Then it grew angry.

"My tree is no longer perfect!" the sultan cried out. "For if it were, it would be blanketed in snow."

At his cry, the other servants came running, the chief steward in the lead. "What is it, O perfect one?"

"That!" the sultan said angrily, pointing to the screen.

"But that is your perfect autumn tree," said the young serving girl, with only the hint of a smile on her face.

"Perfect autumn tree, yes," said the sultan. "But now it is winter."

"Do not be upset, O perfect master," said the chief steward. "We shall make it perfect."

Again the painter was summoned and he labored yet another seven days to paint a perfect winter tree on another panel of the screen, a tree that was blanketed with snow.

And for several months the sultan was delighted with his perfect winter tree.

ut while the sultan gazed with satisfaction at his tree, the world outside had begun to change once more. Little shoots of green were pushing through the brown cover of earth. The trees were wearing buds like delicate green beads.

One day as the sultan sat deep in thought, the young serving girl again entered the room, this time bearing a vase with branches that were covered with young buds and tender green leaves.

"What is this, child?" asked the sultan.

"O perfect master," she said, "pray accept the gardeners' gift of the season."

Again the sultan saw that his tree was no longer perfect, and he cried out in anger. Again the chief steward summoned the painter to paint a new scene. And again, for a few months the sultan was happy.

"Then what shall we do?" cried the chief steward, as much to himself as to the painter. He sat down by the sultan's great canopied bed and wept, his face in his hands.

"If we cannot make a perfect tree, the sultan will not eat or drink. And if he does not eat or drink, he will surely waste away and die."

The painter sat down by his side and wept likewise, for he loved the perfect sultan and did not wish to see him waste away and die.

One by one, as they heard the weeping, the serving men and women came into the room, listened to the sad tale, and sat down beside the chief steward and cried. Soon there was a whole row of them, sitting and sighing and weeping for want of a perfect tree.

But one day, as the sultan sat in perfect contentment, the young servant girl brought him yet another vase filled with fully green boughs and ripe fruit. As she moved toward the table, the branches in the vase bobbed and swayed with their burden.

Neither the sultan nor the girl exchanged a word this time, but when she had gone, the sultan looked over at the screen, his heart heavy in his breast. With several sharp claps of his hand, he called the chief steward to him.

"The tree on my screen is no longer perfect," the sultan said sadly. "It is not fully green and laden with fruit. It does not bend and sway with the weight of its burden. Its imperfection rests heavily on my heart," he confided. "I will not eat or drink until I have a perfect tree."

The chief steward sent for the painter at once. "The tree you painted is no longer perfect," he explained. "This time, our perfect sultan requires a tree that will bend and sway with the weight of its ripe fruit. Only then will it be perfect."

The painter looked downcast. "What you ask, alas, I cannot do. I am a painter, not a god. With my paints, I can make a perfect tree—perfect *for the moment*. But I cannot make it live. I cannot make it grow. I cannot make it change."

"Then what shall we do?" cried the chief steward, as much to himself as to the painter. He sat down by the sultan's great canopied bed and wept, his face in his hands.

"If we cannot make a perfect tree, the sultan will not eat or drink. And if he does not eat or drink, he will surely waste away and die."

The painter sat down by his side and wept likewise, for he loved the perfect sultan and did not wish to see him waste away and die.

One by one, as they heard the weeping, the serving men and women came into the room, listened to the sad tale, and sat down beside the chief steward and cried. Soon there was a whole row of them, sitting and sighing and weeping for want of a perfect tree.

t last the new young serving girl came in and saw the rows of weeping servants. When she, too, had heard the tale, she said, "Oh, you perfect sillies! I know how to make such a tree. It is perfectly simple."

"How can you know ," the chief steward asked his daughter sharply, "when the sultan who is the perfect master, the painter who is the perfect painter, and we who are the perfect servants do not know?"

"Perhaps it is because I am not yet perfect," said the young girl, "for to be perfect means the end of growing. Close your eyes and you shall see."

They all did as they were told—even the chief steward—and the young serving girl went over to the window. Carefully, she took down the folding screen. Outside, the real tree at the garden's center was covered with fruit, and, with every passing breeze, its leaves fluttered and its branches bent and bowed.

"Now you may open your eyes," she said.

The servants opened their eyes and gazed at the place where the screen had been. They saw out into the garden and looked upon the real tree. "Oh!" they all cried.

The chief steward and the painter opened their eyes and saw the tree. "Aah!" they both sighed.

At that, the sultan opened his eyes. He sat up in his bed. Slowly, he rose and went over to the window. For a long, long time he gazed out at the tree. He saw how some of the branches were nearly full and some nearly empty. He saw how some of the branches were short and some long. He saw how some of the branches were almost all green and how some were almost all brown.

"It is not perfect," he said softly.

The servants began to murmur worriedly. The chief steward looked over at his daughter, an angry scowl beginning to crease his handsome brow. But the sultan cut all this short with a wave of his hand.

"It is not perfect," he said, "but it is living, and growing, and changing. That is better than perfect!"

Then he took the young serving girl by the hand and, together, they went out of the palace into the garden to enjoy the fruit of the tree.